JANE THAYER

PICTURES BY SEYMOUR FLEISHMAN

William Morrow and Company
New York 1978

Library of Congress Cataloging in Publication Data

Woolley, Catherine.
    Gus was a gorgeous ghost.

Summary: Gus determines that ghosts needn't always wear white.
[1. Ghost stories] I. Fleishman, Seymour. II. Title.
PZ7.W882Gug 1978   [E]   77-22203
ISBN 0-688-22133-5
ISBN 0-688-32133-X lib. bdg.

Printed in the United States of America.

First Edition
1   2   3   4   5   6   7   8   9   10

For Margot with love

Gus was a fussy old ghost
 so he put on a clean white sheet every day.
He wore his linen sheet,
which was only a hundred years old,
on Monday, Wednesday, and Sunday,
and the homespun sheet,
two hundred years old, the other days.
His residence was an attic apartment,
where he roomed with Cora the cat
and Mouse the mouse.

Each day he lugged the next day's sheet
downstairs to the washing machine.
He spun it in the dryer.
Then he lugged it back up
and ironed it.
He kept the clean sheet
in a ghostly chest.

But ironing gave Gus a backache,
and one day he had a revolutionary idea.
He remarked to Cora,
"Some people use drip-dry sheets."
Cora blinked her yellow eyes. "Buy one."
Gus peered into his shoulder bag.
"Not a ghostly cent.
I'll have to sell my homespun."
He advertised:

Valuable antique homespun sheet for well-dressed ghost.

A rich ghost
named Madame Richardson Richardson,
who wore only handmade sheets,
snapped up this prize.

Her money was in ducats of the year 1200,
but Gus got the ducats changed into dollars
at the Second National Bank.
He put the money in his shoulder bag
and went shopping.
This will save me a lot of work,
he thought with satisfaction,
as he picked out a queen-size
drip-dry sheet.
He put the sheet on then and there.
Needs fitting through the shoulders,
he noted, as he looked in a mirror.

He was on his way out of the store
when he stopped short.
There was another counter
of drip-dry sheets,
but they were so different
from the sheets he was used to
that he couldn't believe they were sheets.
There were pink sheets, yellow, blue,
some with sweet peas.
"I thought sheets
were always white!"
gasped Gus.
He stood there
feasting his eyes,
and then he knew
that he wanted
one of those
beautiful sheets
more than anything
in the world.

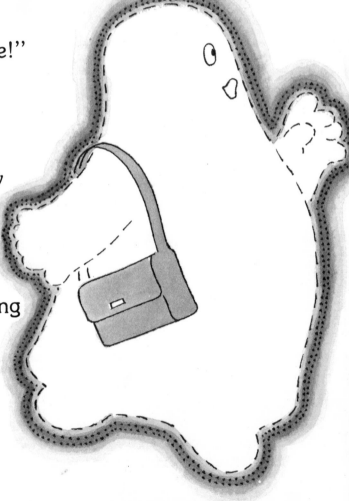

"But ghosts wear
white sheets,"
he moaned.
"The Laws of
Ghostdom say
we wear white sheets!"
He drew his plain white
drip-dry sheet about him,
resisting temptation,
and left without looking back.
So Gus had his drip-dry sheet
and put the ironing board away,
but the sheet gave him no pleasure.
He dreamed he was wearing
a lavender sheet, all lilacs,
and the other ghosts put him in jail.

He peered at himself in a mirror
and looked at the white linen sheet
in the chest.
"I hate white sheets, even drip-dry,"
muttered Gus, and banged down the lid.
Mouse, who had just got married,
was underneath,
chewing a hole in the chest to make a nest.
He nearly fainted from fright.

"Believe me, Cora," said Gus,
"I bitterly resent
having to be plain white
just because I'm a ghost.
I have a right
to some color and beauty in my life!"

He became very cross,
which was not like Gus.
When he happened to step on Cora's tail,
he blamed Cora,
and when Cora sharpened her claws
on the furniture just slightly,
he shouted, "Stop it, stupid!"
"He's going berserk," said Cora.
Mouse almost, not quite, flounced off
to chew a hole somewhere else.

Since he now felt his life
had no color or beauty,
Gus lost interest in life.
He wore his drip-dry sheet all the time,
but he didn't bother to wash it.
He didn't have it fitted
through the shoulders.
He drooped in his chair
and stared into space
and let the days drag by.

Cora felt sorry,
but she had affairs to attend to.
She had to slip out and slip in
and catch up on sleep and sing solos.
She had to find
a mouse or two to munch.
Not Mouse—just some mouse
she didn't know.

Mouse went on chewing the chest.
One snowy night,
no night for cats to go out,
Cora pointed her ears at the chest
and remarked, "Mouse."
Gus didn't hear.
Cora yelled, "Mouse chewing sheet!"
Gus sighed and got out of his chair.
He never wore that linen sheet now,
but he might need it,
so he raised the lid
and took it out.
Underneath skulked Mouse,
furious at being found.
Also Ms. M.
and six children.

"Leave!" thundered Gus,
and he and Cora watched
while Mr. and Ms. Mouse
lugged little ones away.
Then Gus noticed a yellowed paper,
lying on the bottom of the chest.
"What's this?" He took it out.

"Why, it's the Laws of Ghostdom!
I haven't seen these
for at least six hundred years."
He studied some faded words,
and suddenly he cried, "Cora!"
He read aloud, "Article I, Section I.
Ghosts shall go properly clad in sheets."

Gus gasped.

"It doesn't say white sheets!
Then why," he asked in bewilderment,
"do ghosts always wear white?"
The answer came to him.
"I see!" said Gus, nodding wisely.
"White sheets were all they had
when the Laws were laid down.
But since it doesn't say white, Cora,
I can wear a beautiful *colored* sheet!"
He paused. "I haven't got a ghostly cent,
but maybe Madame Richardson Richardson
will buy my linen."
Alas, Madame Richardson Richardson
now wanted no sheet she had to iron.
"I'll give a concert
and raise some money!" Gus cried.
He cleaned the rust off the chains
he kept for occasional clankings
and gave a bang-clank concert.
Cora sang.

But only a few ghosts came,
and even Madame Richardson Richardson
slipped out without paying.

Gus was desperate for money.
"I'll be a night watchman!"
He made a sign, *Beware of Ghosts*,
and haunted a house
whose people were taking a trip.

No sooner had he left at daybreak
than some burglar stole the TV.

But Gus was not going to settle
for an old white sheet now.
"Quiet while I think," he ordered Cora.
Finally he said, "It's simple.
I'll draw pink sweet peas
on my drip-dry sheet with crayons."
He found some crayons
and drew pink sweet peas all over his sheet.
But Cora sat on some,
and when Gus washed off her paw prints
the sweet peas washed off too.
"Very well," said Gus,
and he tried watercolors.
He painted lilacs.
But again the colors ran
in the washing machine.

"I'll Take Lessons
in decorating drip-dry sheets!"
Gus resolved, gritting his teeth.
He went off and Took Lessons
and came home murmuring, "Potato prints."
With ghostly words
Gus produced potatoes for potato prints.
He added some apples,
lemons, carrots, tomatoes, and onions.
Cora was mystified.

Gus collected tubes
of printer's ink and tools.
He spread out his sheet.
Then he mixed the inks until he had
colors that satisfied his soul.
He sliced through his vegetables neatly
and cut clever designs.
No sweet peas this time.
Gus had learned that he should express
his ghostly personality.

He brushed green ink on potatoes
and stamped designs
that had secret meanings for ghosts.
Then he let himself go.
He swooped an onion about
to make a swirling purple mist.
A tomato created blue fog
and mysterious scarlet shadows.
Gus grew bolder and bolder.
He stamped weird creatures
with an apple core.

Strange footprints
in crimson.
An orange owl
whooing a pink whoo.
A broomstick,
a bat,
a witch's brew,
a witch's hat.
Skeletons
in a graveyard
and spooks.

"How's that?" asked Gus,
and while his designs dried
he got the ironing board out
to set the colors with the iron.
Then Gus donned
his decorated drip-dry sheet
and looked in the mirror.
"I have color and beauty
in my life at last!"
he said with a sigh of joy.
He had ink and potatoes left
so he stamped mysterious designs
on his linen sheet, slipcover,
draperies, apron, and walls.
"But I think," Gus said thoughtfully,
"I should explain this
to Madame Richardson Richardson
and all my other friends
who live in a ghostly white world."

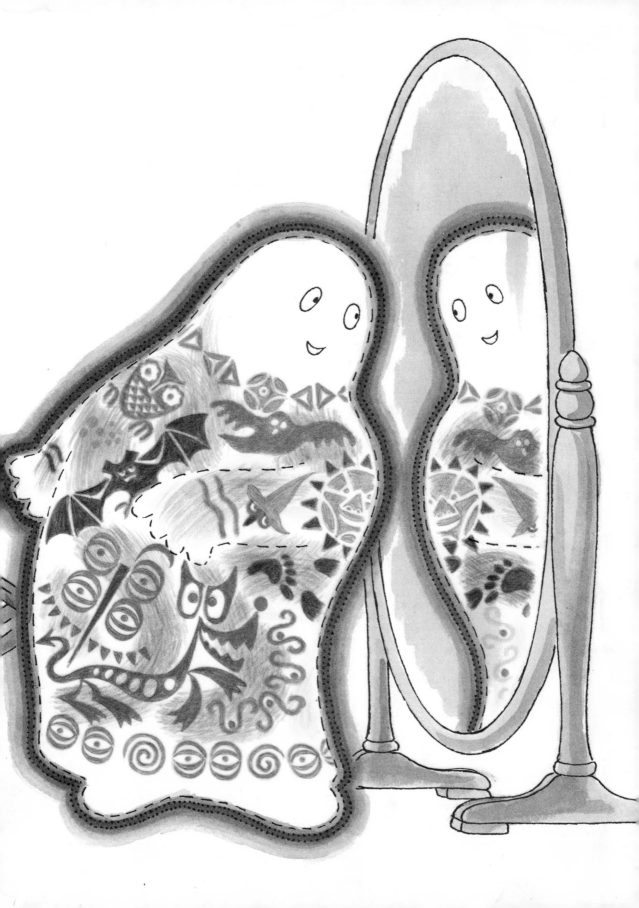

He called a meeting
and read them the Laws of Ghostdom,
which all the ghosts had forgotten.
By unanimous vote they amended
Article I, Section I to read,
"Ghosts shall go clad
in colored sheets if they want to."

When the meeting adjourned,
Gus swept out at once
to have his colorful, colorfast,
decorated drip-dry sheet
fitted through the shoulders.
After that he gave
Madame Richardson Richardson
a lesson in potato prints.